The Ship-Shape Shop

The Ship-Shape Shop

Frank Rodgers

PUFFIN BOOKS

On Saturday mornings Janet and Sam, with Granny and
Mum and Dad, loved to go into town and look at the shops.
One of their favourites was Salty's Junk Shop which was filled
with bits and pieces from old ships.
"Oh, I love this place, Salty," laughed Granny. "It reminds me
of the seaside."

Salty smiled. "Ah, yes," he said. "It's almost as nice as being a sailor again, on my old boat the *Flying Fish*."

Sam pointed to a photograph in the shop window.
"Is that your boat, Salty?" he asked.
"It is indeed, matey," sighed Salty. "She's still there by the seaside where I left her many years ago."
"What are you going to do with your boat, Salty?" asked Janet.
Salty sighed again. "I suppose she'll have to go to the breaker's yard eventually," he said mournfully.

Mrs Grimbly-Whyte, the family's snooty next-door neighbour, was passing and heard this. She stopped and sniffed. "And that is precisely what should happen to this disgraceful old shop if you ask me!" she said. "Someone should knock it down before it falls down."

"But it's full of interesting old things," protested Granny.
"Yes, like me," said Salty, and he and Granny laughed.
Mrs Grimbly-Whyte sniffed again. "You wouldn't catch me having one of those bits of junk in my house. I only buy new antiques. I'm going to inform the Town Council about the state of this shop!"

Mrs Grimbly-Whyte did tell the Town Council and the following week they came and looked at Salty's shop.

On Saturday the family arrived to find Salty looking very glum. "What's wrong, Salty?" asked Granny.
Salty sighed. "The Town Council says my shop is in danger of falling down. If I can't repair it by the end of the week they're going to demolish it."

"Are you going to repair it, Salty?" asked Sam.
"Can't afford to, matey," replied Salty.
"What a shame!" cried Janet, but Granny rolled up her sleeves.
"Never say die, Janet," she said. "That's my motto. We'll help Salty to repair his old shop!"

So the family set to work. They patched the holes in the walls, mended the leaky roof, fixed the rattling windows and painted the front.

Salty was delighted.
"Well," he said. "It certainly looks all ship-shape and Bristol fashion now!"
(Which is an old sailor's way of saying it was neat and tidy.)

But Mrs Grimbly-Whyte didn't think it was ship-shape at all. "It still looks as if it should be pulled down before it falls down!" she snorted.

Unfortunately the Town Council felt the same way. They had a good look at all the repairs and shook their heads. "We're sorry," they said, "but your shop is still not safe. It will have to be demolished."

So the family helped Salty to move all of the stuff out of the
shop and into their garage.

At the end of the week a bulldozer arrived. Salty, Granny and the family watched sadly as, with a thunderous roar, it completely flattened the old shop.

Mrs Grimbly-Whyte stopped on her way past and sniggered. "It certainly doesn't look much like a ship-shape shop now, does it?" she said, and went away smirking.

Granny snapped her fingers. "A ship-shape shop!" she exclaimed. "That's what you'll have, Salty!" Salty was puzzled. "How can I have a ship-shape shop if I don't have a shop, m'dear?" he asked.

"Ah!" said Granny mysteriously. "But you *do* have one, Salty!"

And she whispered her plan to everyone.

That evening Salty, Granny and the family drove down to the seaside.

And later they drove back, pulling something rather large on their trailer.

A few days later, Mrs Grimbly-Whyte passed the spot where
Salty's shop had been and saw that a large curtain of plastic
sheeting had been put up. From behind it came the sound of
hammering and sawing.

"Oh, goody!" she exclaimed. "They are putting up something
new already. Perhaps it will be a nice, clean antiques
supermarket! I think I'll just take a teensy peep inside."

Mrs Grimbly-Whyte looked behind the curtain and got the shock of her life.

"Oh!" she gasped. She couldn't believe her eyes. In place of Salty's old and rather odd junk shop was something older and even more odd!

A ship-shape shop! The family had brought Salty's boat from the seaside and turned it into a wonderful shop for him.

Granny had even made a ship-shape shop sign. It said: THE
ONE AND ONLY SHIP-SHAPE SHOP.

Mrs Grimbly-Whyte was fuming.
"Don't you like it?" asked Granny.
"Like it?" shrieked Mrs Grimbly-Whyte. "It's worse than the last one! I'm going to tell the Town Council about this!" and off she stalked.
"There's no pleasing everyone, is there?" said Granny, and Salty laughed as he took down the screen.

But Janet and Sam were
worried.
"Suppose the Town Council
don't like the Ship-Shape
Shop either," Sam whispered.
"You're right. We've got to
do something," Janet
whispered back.

"We must get some people on our side," she said. "Come on,
I have an idea." And they both slipped quietly into the shop.

A few minutes later Janet and Sam were marching down the street. Sam had an old ship's bell that he rang as loudly as he could.

Janet had an old ship's loudhailer and between them they carried the ship-shape sign. As they marched along Janet called, "Come and see the Ship-Shape Shop! The fabulous, wonderful Ship-Shape Shop!"

A few curious people began to follow them and by the time
they got back to the shop they had gathered a big crowd.

Just then, Mrs Grimbly-Whyte arrived with the people from
the Town Council. They didn't seem very pleased. She elbowed
her way through the crowd and pointed at the Ship-Shape
Shop triumphantly.
"There!" she crowed. "Hideous, isn't it?"

But a lady in the crowd cried out, "No it isn't! I think it's lovely. It reminds me of the seaside!"

"Me too!" said someone else.
"Yes! It's wonderful!" said another.
"Terrific!" said yet another, and everyone joined in.
"Great! Stupendous! Marvellous! Amazing!"

The crowd cheered and gave the Ship-Shape Shop a round of applause. "It's just what this town needs," they said.

The people from the Town
Council agreed.
"This shop won't fall
down. It's as solid as
a rock," they said. "We
think it's wonderful. It
reminds us of our holidays
by the sea too!"

Salty was overjoyed.
"Three cheers for Janet and Sam!" he cried.
"And three cheers for Granny!" cried Janet and Sam.
Granny smiled. "Never say die," she said. "That's my motto."
Mrs Grimbly-Whyte ground her teeth and stomped off.

Lots of people from the town came to help after that, and a few days later Salty had a special opening ceremony for the one and only Ship-Shape Shop.
"It's lovely to be back on my old boat again," he said, and presented Janet and Sam with a ship in a bottle each and Granny with a little statue of a mermaid.

"I'm sure you won't mind, Salty," Granny said, "but I think
Mrs Grimbly-Whyte should have this for her house. After all,
she was the one who gave me the idea for the Ship-Shape
Shop in the first place."
Everyone applauded and for once Mrs Grimbly-Whyte didn't
know what to say.

Salty's Ship-Shape Shop became one of the sights of the town.
Especially during the Town Fair when everybody dressed up
as pirates.

Salty let the children climb all over the Ship-Shape Shop and
pretended he was the Pirate king.
Granny, of course, was the Pirate queen.

"I always wanted to be a sailor," she said. "Maybe next time I'll build a time-machine and travel back to pirate times!" Nobody laughed, because they knew that with Granny nothing was impossible!